Raven: **Gaagaagi**
(gaw-GAW-gi)

Rabbit: **Waabooz**
(WAW-boose)

RAVEN, RABBIT, DEER

by Sue Farrell Holler

Illustrated by
Jennifer Faria

pajamapress

I drop my boots on Grandpa's lap.

"Want to go for a walk?" he asks.

I hold Grandpa's hand so he doesn't fall down or get lost. A truck and a bus and a car stop to let us cross the road.

A big bird with black feathers stands
on the back of a bench.

"**Raven**," says Grandpa. "**Gaagaagi.**"

Raven says, "Hello. Hello."

Raven sounds like the brook in summertime.

My boots make deep holes in the snow.

I shake the prickly hand of a tree.
The snow shower tickles my face
and creeps cold down my neck.

We go around the curve and down the hill and over the wee bridge. The beaver house looks like a lump of snow.

I show Grandpa how to kick snow into the bit of water under the bridge.

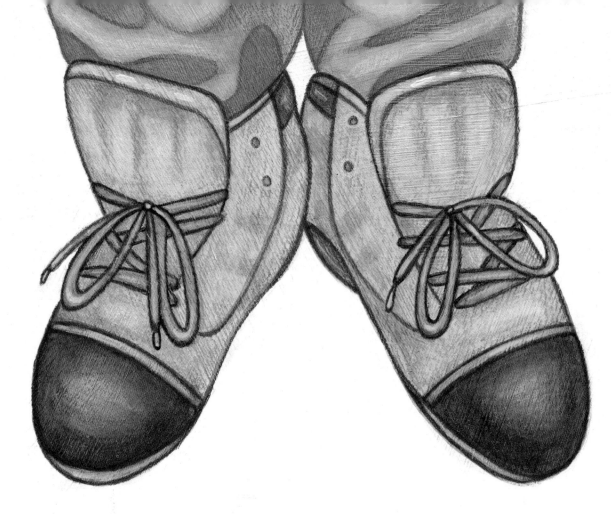

Grandpa puts the heel parts of his
boots together. His boots make a "V."

I copy him and we trudge up the
hill like tractors. Big tractors go
very slowly and puff out a lot of
steam. Little tractors go fast.

We look back. I see tracks of one big tire and one little tire lined up exactly together.

I see marks in the snow that look like two hot dogs with two marshmallows in the middle, then two more hot dogs with two marshmallows.

"**Rabbit**," says Grandpa. "**Waabooz**."

I hop like a bunny. Grandpa doesn't hop.
He watches.

An animal hides in the trees.
It is as still as a picture and
it looks at me.

I point so Grandpa
can see. "Dog," I say.

"**Deer**," says Grandpa.
"**Waawaashkeshi**."
"How many do you see?"

I see one deer. Then the twitch of a tail. Another deer. I see one and one and one more.

I hold up my mitten. "This many," I say.

"Yes," says Grandpa. "Five."

"The one with the antlers is
a boy, like you," he says.

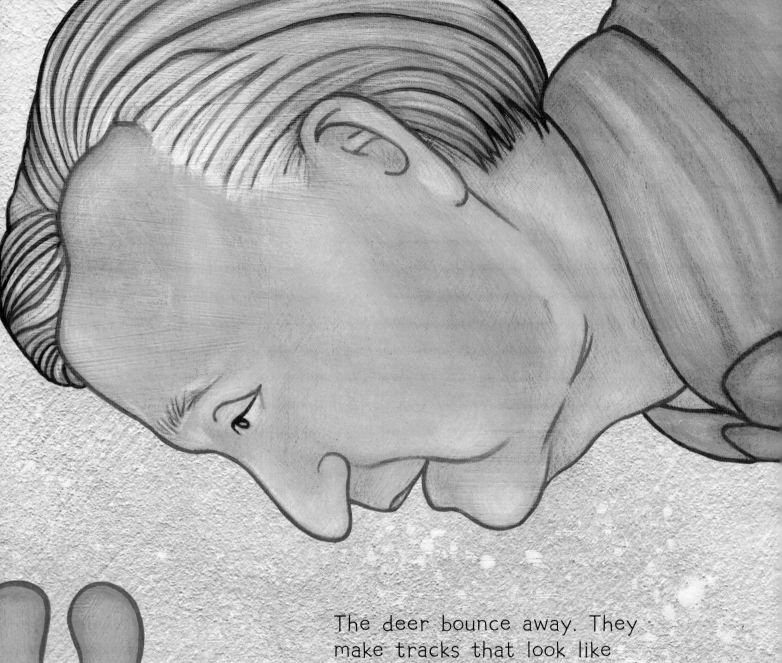

The deer bounce away. They
make tracks that look like
"I love you" hearts cut in two.

I find a line of teeny tiny tracks that look like twigs.

"Bird," says Grandpa.

"Raven," I say. "Gaagaagi."

"Sparrow," says Grandpa. "Sparrow is raven's friend. It has much smaller feet than raven."

Grandpa's face is red and his eyebrows have frost when we get home. He doesn't want to roll like a log in the snow, or dig like a dog, or jump up and down.

He carries me to go inside
like a pile of firewood.

My face tingles and the snow on
my boots turns into a puddle.

Grandpa puts two plates and two
glasses on the table.

He pours the heavy milk.

I get the raisin cookies—a big one
for him and a small one for me.

Grandpa switches the plates.
"Big kids get big cookies," he says.

We sit in Grandpa's chair, ready for reading time. He falls asleep before the end

I slide a blanket over
him, then I snuggle
close to keep him safe.

First published in Canada and the United States in 2020

Text copyright © 2020 Sue Farrell Holler
Illustration copyright © 2020 Jennifer Faria
This edition copyright © 2020 Pajama Press Inc.
This is a first edition.

10 9 8 7 6 5 4 3 2 1

Canada Council   Conseil des arts
for the Arts   du Canada

ONTARIO ARTS COUNCIL
CONSEIL DES ARTS DE L'ONTARIO
an Ontario government agency
un organisme du gouvernement de l'Ontario

Canadä

The publisher gratefully acknowledges the support of the Canada Council for the Arts and the Ontario Arts Council for its publishing program. We acknowledge the financial support of the Government of Canada through the Canada Book Fund (CBF) for our publishing activities.

Library and Archives Canada Cataloguing in Publication

Title: Raven, rabbit, deer / by Sue Farrell Holler ; illustrated by Jennifer Faria.
Names: Holler, Sue Farrell, 1962- author. | Faria, Jennifer, 1979- illustrator.
Identifiers: Canadiana 20200238620 | ISBN 9781772781366 (hardcover)
Classification: LCC PS8615.O437 R38 2020 | DDC jC813/.6—dc23

Publisher Cataloging-in-Publication Data (U.S.)

Names: Holler, Sue Farrell, 1962-, author. | Faria, Jennifer, illustrator.

Title: Raven, Rabbit, Deer / by Sue Farrell Holler, illustrated by Jennifer Faria.

Description: Toronto, Ontario Canada : Pajama Press, 2020. | Summary: "A little boy spends the day with his grandfather, endearingly imagining himself to be the caregiver. On a walk through the forest, the grandfather teaches him to identify a number of animals and their tracks: raven, rabbit, deer and sparrow. Back at the house, their special time ends with milk, cookies, and story time that turns into a nap. Ojibwemowin translations of the animal names are included"— Provided by publisher.

Identifiers: ISBN 978-1-77278-136-6 (hardback)

Subjects: LCSH: Grandfathers -- Juvenile fiction. | Animal tracks -- Juvenile fiction. | BISAC: JUVENILE FICTION / Family / Multigenerational. | JUVENILE FICTION / People & Places / Canada / Indigenous. | JUVENILE FICTION / Science & Nature / Environment

Classification: LCC PZ7.H655Ra |DDC [E] - dc23

Ojibwemowin translations and pronunciations provided by Janice Simcoe, a member of the Chippewas of Rama First Nation

Original art created with acrylic and colored pencil
Cover and book design—Rebecca Bender

Printed in China by WKT Company

Pajama Press Inc.
181 Carlaw Ave. Suite 251 Toronto, Ontario Canada, M4M 2S1

Distributed in Canada by UTP Distribution
5201 Dufferin Street Toronto, Ontario Canada, M3H 5T8

Distributed in the U.S. by Ingram Publisher Services
1 Ingram Blvd. La Vergne, TN 37086, USA

Grandpa introduces his forest neighbors in English and Ojibwemowin.

Deer: **Waawaashkeshi**
(WAW-wash-kay-shi)